I0760914

Double O 54

By Fern Best

Double O 54

First Edition 2023

Library and Archives Canada
ISBN
Paperback 978-1-998245-08-6
Hardcover 978-1-998245-07-9

Book design by Kabrena L. Robinson
Published by Eva-Michelle & Family Publishing
www.evamichelleandfamily.com

Contents

Double O 54

Each year, many brave little warriors are admitted to hospitals facing serious illnesses; illnesses most can't even pronounce. It's a lonely and scary time for them, especially when their families can't be by their side. But these little ones are survivors. There may be no medicine for loneliness, but there definitely is a recipe to prevent it, and good friends and family are the main ingredients. Join the adventures of Double O 54, a crew of 'hospital kids' who refuse to let their illnesses get them down. They embark on wild adventures, full of twists and turns that only race car drivers could handle, and mysteries that only super sleuths could solve. Join them as they spread joy and laughter, proving that even in the toughest of times, happiness can be found if you have good friends by your side. Double O 54; they're like Double O 7, but cooler.

CHAPTER 1

The Phantom Gang

Fuchsia stared through the window to the crowded parking lot below. In the corner of her eye, she could see her mom checking her watch and looking at the door where the doctor was supposed to appear some forty-five minutes ago.

This was not new. She had been sick before and had to stay in the hospital several times, but this time was different. She overheard the nurse telling her mom that it was not going to be just overnight; it might be longer.

For as long as she could remember, she was sick. Chills and lightheadedness were the main symptoms, but lately, it had gotten worse. She was so tired all the time and had difficulty breathing.

She had not played with her friends in over a year, especially since COVID, and now the doctor who had finally arrived, was at the door telling her mom that she would need a new kidney. She watched as her mom listened and saw the tears gleaming in her eyes. This was bad. Her mom was calmly nodding her head, but Fuchsia knew she was crying inside. When the doctor left, her mom walked slowly to her bed as if the burden was simply too much. Her mom tucked her in and glanced at her watch again. Fuchsia knew how hard it was for her mom to leave, but knew she needed to work and take care of her little brother.

"You have to leave now if you are going to pick up Draymond on time Mom. Go, I'll be alright," Fuchsia said with as much cheer as she could muster.

"I know, but I don't want to leave you alone," her mom replied.

"Don't worry, Dad will be here soon, and I am going to sleep anyway. See you when you get back," and with that, Fuchsia closed her eyes and pretended to sleep.

Her mom kissed her on the forehead, squeezed her hand and then tip-toed out of the room, wiping her eyes.

When the door finally closed, Fuchsia opened her eyes and resumed looking at the car park. There were pigeons and black birds flying about and a few squirrels racing up and down the trees. How free they all looked and not at all tired like she was.

From the corner of her eye, there was movement. It wasn't a doctor or a nurse, and way too short to be her mom coming back. There, she saw it again. A reflection in the door caught her attention. She could see someone in a wheelchair, and someone standing on the back trying to peek through the door. She closed her eyes and pretended to sleep. Who could these people be? She had nothing to steal and they looked no older than she was, so where were their parents? She heard the door open and the slight squeak of wheels coming closer to her bed.

"I think she is asleep," one voice said. It was a girl. She was wearing a hospital gown over her clothes and a knitted cap over her very short hair.

"Are you sure this is the one you heard Nurse Anita talking about?" The second voice came from the chair. It was a little hoarse and very raspy, and he was breathing heavily.

"That's what the chart says," the girl responded.

Did she just look at my chart? Fuchsia's mind screamed. *That's it!* From her position on her bed and without opening her eyes Fuchsia shouted, "You have five seconds to leave this room, or I will call security."

The boy in the wheelchair started to breathe faster, "Oh boy, let's get out of here!"

"Five, four, three…" Fuchsia started her countdown and grabbed the phone to show she meant business.

"Oh, stop your bellyaching," the girl said flatly. "I am Phantom, and this here is Kevin. Consider us your welcome committee."

"Welcome committee to what, a hospital?" Fuchsia rebutted. "Please, there is no such thing. You have two seconds. I am dialling… two, one"

"Ok, ok, we are leaving. No problem; you will be here for a while anyway. So, if you get lonesome, come look for us on Ward 54." She left a paper on her tray, hopped on the back of Kevin's wheelchair and left.

Fuchsia put down the phone and picked up the paper. She didn't know the number for security anyway. The paper was a hand-written invitation. *Who would want an invitation to stay in a hospital,* she thought. She crumpled the paper, throwing it into the wastebasket.

Fuchsia closed her eyes for real this time. She missed home but didn't want to complain. She replied to some messages from her aunties and uncles on her phone, accepting their well wishes and prayers, but still felt lonely. Her eyes then fell on the paper in the wastebasket.

Fishing it out, she read it remembering her two intruders. *What kind of name was Phantom anyway?* Curiosity and boredom got the best of her, so she grabbed her walker and decided to investigate. There were a few stares from nurses, but she continued slowly towards Ward 54.

She was finally there. Through the door, she could hear talking and laughing. What kind of ward was this? She asked herself.

She opened the door and was startled as a nurse was right there. She thought she was in trouble, but the nurse just smiled, winked and nodded her head in the direction of the laughter.

"Hello?" Fuchsia called out in a timid voice. The laughter ceased and the curtain that separated the beds opened slightly.

"Hello?" she called again. This time the curtain opened fully to show a group of children around a bed. Some had short hair, some had no hair, some had bandages and tubes, but all had big smiles. Then, there was Phantom in the middle.

"Nice of you to join us, Fuchsia," she said as if she was chairing a board meeting.

Fuchsia was a little shocked that Phantom used her name but then remembered her looking at her chart.

"You remember Kevin," she continued. This is Sarge, short for Sergeant. This is Mac, short for MacGyver and this is Pic, short for Picasso. We are the Phantom Gang."

"No, we are not!" Everyone shouted out in unison.

"I told you to stop saying that," Sarge spoke up. "We decided to go with Double O 54."

"Yeah, like Double O 7, but better," Kevin chimed in.

"Whatever, Phantom Gang," Phantom repeated unperturbed.

"Sarge, Mac, Pic, … are those even your real names?" Fuchsia asked, trying not to sound too interested.

"No silly, those are our superpowers," Phantom clarified.

"Your what?" Fuchsia chuckled.

Sarge jumped in, "Well, we have been here, in and out, for some time now. We know how difficult it is to be alone in a hospital so we have made it our mission to use our talents to welcome new arrivals and let them know that God loves them and that no matter what, they will be ok."

"Okay, let me guess," Fuchsia started to warm up to them, "Sarge is in charge."

"I *am* the oldest," Sarge declared, stressing heavily on the "am" for emphasis and receiving eye rolls from Phantom.

"MacGyver makes things?" Fuchsia continued.

"He is a genius; he doesn't speak much but he created our communication system," she explained, pointing to walkie-talkies and a box of odd-looking gadgets, some tin cans and cords.

"Okay … and Picasso paints?" Fuchsia asked cautiously.

"He is visual communication," replied Phantom. "Pictures, postcards, you name it."

"And what pray tell does a Phantom do?" Fuchsia asked.

"Phantoms 'pray tell', gets in and out of places without being seen, Phantom retaliated mockingly. I know every inch of this place."

Everyone then looked at Kevin. "And, what does a Kevin do?" Fuchsia asked. With a big toothy smile, he huffed, "I am transportation."

Everyone laughed, including Fuchsia.

"So Double O 54 huh? What kind of 'gang' is this?" Fuchsia asked.

From behind Pic's back came a banner. "We were actually planning a party to cheer you up. We have a banner, games and snacks," Sarge explained.

"And I know where to get my hands on some chocolate pudding," Phantom joined in when suddenly, the door opened.

"There you are!" It was Fuchsia's dad. "What are you doing out of bed? I couldn't find you and your mom was on the phone having a fit."

"Sorry Dad," Fuchsia apologized, "I needed to stretch my legs." She was about to explain further when Phantom put a finger to her lips and mouthed the words "See you at seven o'clock."

Fuchsia went back to her room. She loved hanging with Dad. He would sneak in her favourite snacks and they would talk and laugh about everyone and everything. At six-thirty, the bell rang, and Dad's face got sad. He kissed her on the forehead, squeezed her hand and told her that she would be okay.

As he was leaving, he spoke to the nurse on duty. The nurse assured him that Fuchsia would be all right and that she would check in on her as soon as she returned from reallocating some elderly patients. Apparently, they were to have a show, but it was cancelled because of the weather. She advised him to leave soon to avoid being caught in the storm.

Dad turned and waved a final goodbye. Fuchsia felt alone again. She started to pray for her Dad to get home safely and for her parents to be happy and also for the disappointed old patients. In the middle of her prayer, she had an idea. She hopped out of bed, and as fast as her walker could take her, headed down the hallway to Ward 54. When she got there, quite out of breath, she told the gang her idea. She told them what she had heard about the weather and the older patients, then advocated that Double O 54 give the old patients her party. They loved the idea. Double O 54 to the rescue!

Sarge got to work mapping out the logistics. Phantom knew exactly how to get there without being seen—with talk about broom closets and stairwells. Picasso decided that he would do caricatures of the old folks, Mac was going to frame them and Phantom and Kevin had a special treat.

The old folks were ecstatic for the company. Sarge had music playing and Phantom and Kevin's "mad modelling and crazy ballet" had them all in stitches. Then, they all came together to record some TikTok dances. Boy, did these old folks have the moves. There were lots of hugs and cheek-pinching, but the gang didn't mind. For the first time in a long time, Fuchsia was happy. She realized that it was making others happy and that put her in a good mood.

Hearing noises in the hallway, Fuchsia flipped the lights three times as she was instructed. It was time to go. They packed up their things and waved goodbye. Just as the nurses were entering, they escaped into an adjoining hallway through what looked like a storage room. Wow! Phantom really knew this place.

When she sneaked back into her room, Fuchsia crawled into bed, she could not remember the last time she was so happily tired. As she closed her eyes to say her prayers, she heard the door open. It was Phantom.

"Just checking to make sure you were okay, and to say thanks for joining Double O 54; we needed another girl," she said laughing.

"Fantasia, is that you?" a voice came from the hallway. It was the nurse.

"Uh oh. Got to go," and with that Phantom, or

Fantasia slipped into the dark hallway and disappeared.

Fuchsia chuckled. She didn't promise to be a part of their gang, but she liked them.

As sleep claimed her tired little body, Fuchsia whispered a prayer, "Lord, bless Double O 54 and Phantom, or Fantasia."

CHAPTER 2

The Phantom Lights

It had been almost a week since Fuchsia's escapade with the 'Phantom' gang. Every time she thought of them, she would giggle until she could hardly breathe. She had been back and forth for all sorts of X-rays and scans and was so weak she could hardly leave her bed. She wondered what they were up to now, and if Phantom, or Fantasia, got caught sneaking out of her room the other night.

As she peered through the window examining what she now considered to be her parking lot, she looked for the black squirrel with the fluffy tail. It was getting colder outside so it was probably behind the hedge searching for food to store up for winter, she thought. She didn't see many birds anymore, but the geese would fly by every morning and evening. They made such a racket overhead that Fuchsia would imagine they were telling her the day's news. In her mind, it sounded like this: *Guess who flew into a window yesterday? Would you believe that Lucy Goosey ate that worm? Did you hear that Linda's eggs finally hatched? Look at little Tommy Drake swimming by himself, sure took him long enough!*

Fuchsia could not help but smile at the images swirling around in her head and wondered why in her imagination the geese had a Bronx-Italian accent. God took care of all of them and he will take care of her too.

As these hilarious images ran through her thoughts, she heard a familiar squeak.

"Are you awake?" Kevin's hoarse voice whispered.

Fuchsia looked around, but instead of Phantom, Mac was riding shotgun.

"Hi, guys. Hey, where's Phantom?" Fuchsia asked.

"That's why we are here. She isn't well. They put her in a room by herself for treatment," Kevin answered sadly.

Mac hopped off the back of the chair and started tapping the walls and fiddling with a walkie-talkie.

He handed one to Fuchsia.

"She wants to talk to you," Kevin rasped. "She said it was important, so it must be a girl thing."

With that, Mac hopped on the back of the wheelchair and like a cowboy in a love story, waved goodbye as they left. Fuchsia would have giggled if this didn't sound so serious. She had to talk to Phantom but that evening the whole family came to visit, so Fuchsia hid the walkie-talkie.

She played with her little brother until it was time for them to leave. It was still lonesome without them, but it was getting easier to manage.

As soon as they left and she was sure the nurse wasn't nearby, she pulled out the walkie-talkie. She fiddled with the switches and said, "Hello." There was no response. She even said, "Roger!" like in the movies and with that she got a faint laugh from the other end.

"Phantom. Is that you?" Fuchsia whispered.

"Who else would it be?" Phantom sounded tired but it was the same quick wit.

"How are you?" Fuchsia asked concerned.

"The same as you, that's why we are in a hospital, remember?" Phantom responded. "Anyways, enough about me, we have a case."

"A what?" Fuchsia was lost.

"A case, newbie, and Double O 54 has to solve it." Phantom was insistent. "The gang is meeting here at seven P.M., I need you to come."

From the other end of the walkie-talkie Fuchsia heard the nurse saying "Fantasia, you need your rest!"

"Uh oh, got to go," was the last thing she heard before the click.

What was going on? What was this case Phantom was talking about? Fuchsia looked at the clock. It was almost seven P.M. now. Making sure the nurse was nowhere to be seen, Fuchsia grabbed her walker and hobbled down the corridor. She was almost a hundred meters from her room when it dawned on her that she did not know what room they had put Phantom in, so she peeked at the charts on her way down. None of the charts said Phantom or Fantasia, but one said F. Atom... Fantasia Atom… Phantom; that was close enough. It also said 'Lymphoma'. She had never heard of it before and promised to look it up. Then, there was the tell-tale sound of laughter.

Fuchsia timidly opened the door. It was dark inside. She was about to turn around, thinking that she intruded on a stranger when a lamp flicked on, but there was the gang on the bed.

"So glad you are here, Fuchsia. They won't listen to me and this is serious business," Phantom said with her arms crossed.

Fuchsia took a seat while Phantom explained the predicament.

"Ok, so you are saying to me that in the middle of the night, at exactly eleven o'clock, this light goes on and off, by itself. You are saying you tried but nothing happens when you flip the switch?" Fuchsia summarized.

"Yes!" Phantom sounded frustrated. "I think we are dealing with a case of aliens. They want to abduct me, and Double O 54 has to stop them. I get enough prodding here on earth; I don't want to be part of their experiments."

"Aliens? That's the craziest thing I have ever heard," Sarge countered. "It is most likely to be a short in the wiring or something of the sort."

"Shouldn't be. Mac looked and everything is brand new. This wing was only built a couple of years back," Phantom explained.

"I think it is the ghost of dead children coming to haunt us," Kevin said in a scary voice.

"There is no such thing." Fuchsia spoke up.

"For the living know that they will die but the

dead know nothing," she repeated, quoting the text from Ecclesiastes nine verse five.

"What does that mean?" Picasso whispered as if afraid to seem dumb.

"It means that they do not exist," Phantom added, "unlike aliens."

"But what about the babies crying at the same time? You have to agree that's spooky," Kevin added.

"It is definitely weird," Fuchsia admitted.

"What if it is a signal?" Sarge asked, walking around with a finger tapping on his temple as if he was conjuring up big thoughts. "You said that it flicked three times: short, long, short. What if it was an SOS and someone needs help?"

"Yeah, the souls of those dead children" Kevin tried again but the dirty looks made him zip his lips.

Everyone sat there in silence.

"No offence, Phantom, but we need to see this for ourselves to make sure that you are not making this up," Sarge finally said.

"Offence much?" Phantom retorted. "Anyway," Phantom continued while rolling her eyes.

"How do you expect me to prove it? It happens

in the middle of the night."

"Well, we will have to stay here then," Sarge said, and they all agreed.

Fuchsia looked at the clock. It was now eight o'clock and that meant a three-hour wait.

Normally she would be so tired she would dismiss this and head back to bed, but Phantom looked so pale and scared, Fuchsia wanted to be there for her. Sarge then set the alarm on his watch for ten forty-five; they turned off the lights and settled in for the wait.

In the dark, Fuchsia 'googled' Lymphoma. No wonder Phantom seemed so sick, Lymphoma was a type of cancer. She must have been doing treatments and that was why her hair was so short. Sad at this discovery, Fuchsia turned her attention to the TV. It was showing reruns of *The Golden Girls.* She could hear Kevin wheezing and soft snores from the others.

At some point in time, she dozed off and in the middle of a muddled dream, she found herself with Dorothy and Rose on *The Golden Girls* TV show, who had found a baby. The clock struck eleven o'clock and the baby started to cry. Blanch took it away to feed it, but when she removed the blanket it turned out to be Sophia. When Sophia took out her teeth to suck at the bottle, Fuchsia knew she must have been dreaming. Her grandmother was right; TV does rot your brain. As she was about to tell The Golden Girls that this was all a dream, Sophia let out the biggest burp … and the alarm went off.

Phantom was already up. Sarge was busy waking the others and shushing everyone to be quiet, and quiet it was; deathly quiet. They all sat there secretly counting down the time. Ten fifty-five ... ten fifty-six ... ten fifty-seven ... ten fifty-eight ... ten fifty-nine …

Everyone sat up in anticipation. Eleven o'clock came and still nothing happened.

They stared at each other and started to chuckle. Was all this for nothing? Then, the lights flickered ... one short, one long, one short. Everyone looked at Phantom and gasped. They all gasped even louder when the babies started to cry.

Phantom was right. She had the biggest 'I told you so' look on her pale little face. Sarge jumped up and tried the light switch. Nothing! Something was definitely going on.

The very tired and sleepy Double O 54 met up the next night determined to figure this thing out.

What was causing those lights to flicker like that and why were they hearing babies cry? It was determined that they should follow the wiring to see where it ended up.

The six of them, including Phantom still hooked up to her oxygen and drips, crept from room to room asking patients if they had noticed anything strange; no one had. The group was now beginning to doubt what they had seen, and it was getting late. Deciding to check one more room, they found the 'Baby Ward'. It was dark inside and through the wall of glass, they could see an army of sleeping babies. There was the sound of footsteps and everyone scampered to hide as it was way past bedtime and they would definitely be in trouble. In fact, it was almost eleven o'clock.

They hid behind the wall as a nurse entered the Baby Ward. Commenting on how dark it was, she flicked the light switch. Nothing happened. She flicked it a couple more times and still nothing happened.

"Uhh, are they ever going to fix this light?" the nurse ranted to no one in particular.

Double O 54 looked at each other in the dark. An alarm went off and the babies, as if sensing dinner, started to cry. It was now eleven o'clock.

They crept back to Phantom's room all excited.

Did you hear that? Her light didn't work either. That must be a clue," Phantom said ecstatically.

"Yeah, but it didn't blink like yours though," Sarge pointed out, and she flicked it three times to be sure." Seeing Phantom's downcast face, he quickly added, "but the babies cried at exactly eleven o'clock, that's definitely something."

Phantom looked excited again but that quickly turned to eye rolls when Kevin added in a scary voice, "That's when their souls were being snatched."

"You need to stop watching horrors on TV. That was feeding time, silly, that's why they were crying," Picasso added.

Remembering the dream, a chuckle crept up Fuchsia's throat. *We should all stop watching TV*, she thought.

"The two must be connected," Phantom said desperately. She was beginning to sound weak again.

"Why don't we rest tonight and figure this out tomorrow," Fuchsia volunteered.

Reluctantly, Phantom got into bed and the others left for Ward 54. Fuchsia headed for her room in the other direction, flicking the light switch one more time to see if there was any change. Nothing!

This was indeed puzzling. On the way back she heard maintenance on their radio saying that they were headed to the Baby Ward because the light kept flicking at odd times. Fuchsia stopped in her tracks; that sounded like Phantom's lights. Fuchsia had an idea.

The gang met up the next night, and Fuchsia had the floor. She explained her hypothesis, but they needed to test it. So, armed with walkie-talkies they divided into two groups. Group One consisted of Phantom, Kevin and Mac, who stayed in Phantom's room while Group Two; Sarge, Pic and Fuchsia, headed to the Baby Ward.

Just before eleven o'clock the nurse walked into the room and flicked the light on; one short, one long, one short, she complained. Then, the alarm sounded, and the babies started to cry. There was instantly a crackling from the walkie-talkies and Group One confirmed in a chorus of excited voices that the mysterious lights in Phantom's room just flickered.

It was now Group Two's turn. They got into position to see the Baby Ward as Sarge gave Group One the command. The lights in the Baby Ward flickered. Fuchsia's hypothesis was correct. The light switch from the babies' room somehow controlled Phantom's lights, and the lights switch from Phantom's room controlled the lights in the Baby Ward. Group two hurried back to Phantom's room. There was excitement all around at solving the puzzle and Fuchsia watched as Phantom breathed a sigh of relief.

The next day they were able to tell the maintenance crew and they fixed those lights in no time, shaking their heads for they knew better than to ask the Phantom to explain how she knew this.

That night they met again. Pic had started a Double O 54 diary and they recapped the whole story to be notarized, as Sarge put it.

"I am glad it wasn't aliens," Phantom said amid bouts of laughter. She was feeling better and was to be heading back to Ward 54 soon.

"Aliens? I am glad it wasn't a ghost," Kevin responded with a dramatic shudder.

Everyone looked at Kevin and in unison shouted, "For the dead know nothing!".

That night Fuchsia said a special prayer for her new friends.

"God bless Double O 54, and Phantom... especially Phantom."

CHAPTER 3

The Phantom Family

They all lined up at the door to wave goodbye to Kevin. His asthma was under control and he was heading home. As Fuchsia waved goodbye, she realized how much she was going to miss him and his 'transportation'. She cast her mind back to how they first met and giggled. She was happy that he got to go home but wished it was her who was going home instead; it was a weird mix of emotions.

Fuchsia had since been moved into Ward 54 to 'recover'. She was glad for the company and was getting to know her 'gang' pretty well. Sarge was indeed the oldest. He was from a law enforcement family and wanted to study law. Mac was a quiet darling who did speak, but rarely. His family owned a computer store. He liked fixing things and was the first to volunteer if the nurses complained that something didn't work. Pic went nowhere without his sketch pad. He was often found drawing by the window. He had talent and the ward was decorated with his paintings. It was hard to tell if he was the youngest of the group or Phantom. *Speaking of Phantom, where was she?* Fuchsia thought.

Everyone was eating leftover cake and playing one of Mac's games, but Phantom was off to the corner. Fuchsia was about to make her way over when she caught Sarge's eye. He silently shook his head in a negative way and then beckoned her with a head nod.

"Just leave her be; she will be alright," he said sadly.

"Why?" Fuchsia questioned, "I want to find out what's wrong."

"We all know what's wrong and you would too if you paid attention," he whispered.

"What do you mean?" Fuchsia asked, confused. "I pay attention."

"Not enough or you would notice that Phantom always leaves during visiting hours. So, when we are busy with our families, she has no one."

He was right. Fuchsia had only been in the ward for a couple of days, but she had never seen anyone visit her. Fuchsia was shook. She had been so wrapped up in her own drama, that she hadn't noticed what was right in front of her.

"But Sarge," Fuchsia questioned, "I see her with new toys and snacks all the time. How does she get them if no one visits?"

"She pretty much orders what she wants from her Dad's account and has them delivered. Her mom died when she was little, and I guess he is busy with his new family. In fact, I am sure of it. He is getting remarried this week."

Fuchsia thought about Phantom for the rest of the day. She wanted to cheer her up but didn't know how. During visitation, Fuchsia tried to keep an eye on Phantom and incorporate Phantom into her family conversations, but before she knew it, like her namesake, Phantom had disappeared.

That night, in the middle of a restless sleep, she was awakened by Mac tugging at her sleeve.

"What's wrong Mac? Are you ok? Do you need the nurse?"

"She's gone," Mac replied.

"Who's gone, the nurse? She will be back soon." Fuchsia said, trying to get her sleeping brain to activate.

Mac shook his head and with a surprisingly strong grip pulled her towards Phantom's bed; it was empty.

Fuchsia was suddenly awake and alert by the sight of Phantom's empty bed.

They searched the bathrooms, the closets and even the hallway. There was no sign of Phantom. They realized they needed help. They first woke Sarge and after a brief explanation, he had the others up and assigned to search some of Phantom's hiding places. They looked in the chapel, the kitchen, even the doctor's lounge ... still, no Phantom."

This was serious, especially since this was not the first time Phantom had disappeared. Sarge explained that the last time involved the police and her father had told her that if it happened again, he would put her in another hospital. So, they had to find her before the nurse noticed that she was missing during her morning rounds.

They searched everywhere they could think of … twice; they even went up to the roof and the helicopter pad. Still, no Phantom. It was almost morning and they had to come up with a plan and fast. They decided they would go back to bed and then pretend that this was news to them in the morning to buy some more time to figure things out.

Tired and sleepy, Fuchsia sat on the side of her bed and stared through the window. Luckily, she still had her view of the parking lot but this side was busier. She watched as the emergency personnel wheeled people in. It dawned on her that the hospital was good at healing bodies but not so good at healing hearts and souls. After all, there was no medication for loneliness.

Fuchsia said a prayer for Phantom. She knew she must have been hurting, and to be taken away from her hospital home and away from the only friends she had, would only make it worse.

As Fuchsia opened her tired eyes and stared into the lights of the ambulance, the illumination gave the dreary hospital the vague illusion of happiness and seemed to make the shadows dance. Fuchsia looked closer. It seemed as if this particular shadow was doing more than dancing; it was ducking behind cars and people. Did this shadow look exactly like Phantom, or was there another pale, little girl out there trying to escape?

Fuchsia turned to Sarge for help, but his breathing told her he was already asleep. It was up to her. She grabbed her coat to cover her hospital gown. As she grabbed for her walker it dawned on her that it would only draw unwanted attention, so she left it. Without thinking, she hurried through the ward, peeked into the empty hallway and then hopped into the open elevator. She was almost out of breath, but so far so good.

The short ride opened to the crowded emergency floor. Fuchsia easily moved around the bodies unnoticed and made her way to the exit. She was just in time to see her 'shadow' get into a taxi.

"Phantom!" Fuchsia called, pulling her hood up against the wind. Phantom looked around and recognizing the voice hopped into the taxi which was about to leave. Not knowing what else to do, Fuchsia stepped into the path of the oncoming taxi and with one hand raised, reminiscent of Moses at the Red Sea, and one eye closed, she commanded the taxi to stop.

"Fantasia Atom! Get out this minute or I will call security." The door opened and Phantom reluctantly exited. The frightened taxi driver swerved around her and sped off. This was the second time she threatened to call security for Phantom. Interestingly enough, this time, she didn't even have a phone.

"What were you thinking Phantom?" Fuchsia

angrily asked while ushering Phantom indoors, her body shivering from the cold.

"You don't understand," Phantom said angrily, pulling away.

"What don't I understand ... that I risked my health and not to mention my life to stop you from making a mistake?" Fuchsia responded.

"No! You don't understand. You, Fabulous Fuchsia, with your family to visit you and siblings to play with, you don't understand. I have no one."

Fuchsia knew in an instant that Phantom was right. Her delivery wasn't the most pleasant, but she was right. Her family visited her every day.

"Tell me about your Mom," Fuchsia asked as she ushered the sulking Phantom into the elevator.

"She was beautiful. I barely remember her face, but I remember she always smelled heavenly whenever she hugged me; like baby powder. I only have pictures and her things to remind me of her; that's why I have to go get them. My dad is remarrying and he is throwing her things away. I must get them. It is all I have left of her."

The next day, Phantom's predicament was all the tired, sleepy Double O 54 could talk about. They brainstormed ways that they could help her.

Her father was out of town and not answering

his phone. Her grandparents lived far away, and the truck was to arrive the next day to take the things away. They were all surprised when Picasso volunteered, "Let's go get them."

"What? How? No way!" were the gang's initial responses.

"I don't need everything, just the heirlooms she gave me … my locket, my quilt, my picture books. I mean I do have a key." Phantom added with a pouty mouth and puppy dog eyes, "We could be there and back before visiting hours if we hurry."

They all looked at each other. Within moments a plan was hatched.

Sarge called the taxi company and in his most convincing adult voice, instructed them to pick up his "children" a block away. They decided that Pic and Mac would stay to cover for them, redirect queries from the nursing staff and alert them on Fuchsia's phone if there was trouble.

Sarge, Phantom and Fuchsia bundled up as best as they could and began the journey, which almost ended before it started as Nurse Nita was right outside. They had no idea when she would leave and they didn't want to miss the taxi, so Picasso went ahead to distract her with one of his paintings while the rest of the crew escaped to the elevator.

Outside was colder than they thought, but adrenaline kept them moving. The taxi was running late so they waited by the gate of a nearby house pretending they lived there. When the taxi arrived, they rushed out.

"Are you here to pick up the Atomborough children?" Phantom questioned the taxi driver going along with the plan set in motion by Sarge.

With the affirmative, they waved to their pretend parents and quickly entered the taxi.

They all sat silently throughout the thirty-minute car ride not knowing what to expect. Fuchsia kept checking the phone every five minutes, frightened that they were going to get into trouble.

Arriving at what looked like a mansion surrounded by the most beautiful gardens they got out of the taxi and looked around in amazement. For a moment, Fuchsia wished she was Phantom and got to play there, but then quickly remembered why she was there and took it back. Her family was happy with the little they had.

They asked the taxi to wait while Phantom opened the door. The inside was even more impressive.

They were tempted to look around, but

Phantom quickly marched them up to her room and immediately started filling their arms and any other appendage with things she just couldn't part with. Then the phone rang. Fuchsia was so frightened she dropped the things she was holding. Surely, this was it. They had been caught. They all looked at each other startled; the call was from the hospital.

After the third ring, Phantom mustered the courage to answer. A very anxious Pic was on the other side. Phantom's dad had called the hospital to say that he was coming to visit her, and the nurse wanted to give her the good news. This was not good. They had to get back to the hospital right away. They grabbed all the stuff and headed to the taxi waiting outside. Loaded up and ready to leave, they realized that Phantom was missing.

In desperation, Sarge headed back in with a no-soldier-left-behind look on his face and dragged the bedazzled Phantom out to the car. She was wearing her mother's locket and smiling from ear to ear.

Luckily they made it back to the hospital just in time for visiting hours. Phantom tipped the taxi driver for his 'troubles' and the crew ladened with Phantom's treasures hurried inside. With a sigh of relief and everything stuffed hurriedly into Phantom's cupboard, they went to greet their families. This time Phantom did not disappear as not only her dad but her soon-to-be stepmother and two step sisters arrived. Instantly the story of Cinderella came to Fuchsia's mind although she could not picture anyone bossing about the quick-witted Phantom.

The bell rang all too soon. Fucshia now saw family in a new light and really appreciated her family's effort to visit her every day. They didn't need a big house with lovely gardens to be happy; they just needed each other, she thought.

As the families waved goodbye Fuchsia heard a deep voice speaking to her.

"You must be Fuchsia. I am Fantasia's dad. Thank you for taking care of her while she is here."

Fuchsia looked over at Phantom. It was the happiest she had ever seen her.

"I hear you want to be a counsellor someday. I trust you won't be adding breaking and entering to your resume," he said with a smile.

Fuchsia's eyes opened wide at what he said. She smiled nervously and headed to the back of the room to debrief with the rest of the gang.

That night they brought Mac and Pic up to

speed on all that happened throughout their little adventure. Mac and Pic had a good laugh hearing how they pretended to live at that house and actually pretended to wave goodbye to whomever lived there, and that they were now proud members of the Atomborough Family. Phantom showed them her treasures with the biggest smile while sharing her memories.

"How did your dad know that we went to the house?" Fuchsia chimed in remembering that embarrassing conversation she had with Phantom's dad earlier.

Phantom, with a sly smile, confessed that they had tripped the alarm while there. Her dad had told her he was sorry for not being around and that he would store her mom's things for her. He further assured her that her bedroom and the rest of her family would be waiting for her to come home and from then on, they would be visiting regularly.

Later, five tired Double O 54 bodies hopped in their beds and hurriedly went to sleep. Fuchsia fought sleep enough to thank God for protecting them that day and asked forgiveness for the little "untruths" they told to help Phantom, who now had the family she needed.

There was still no medicine for loneliness but there definitely was a recipe to prevent it, and good friends and family were the main ingredients.

CHAPTER 4

The Phantom List

"Shhh!" Sarge signalled for the group to be quiet. They were all crowded into the closet with literally no room to breathe much less move. They were on a mission led by Phantom but ran into unexpected hospital personnel. *How do I get myself into these situations?* Fuchsia thought, but then giggled to herself as she looked over at Phantom and Double O 54.

When the coast was clear, they exploded into the adjourning hallway. They were on a floor Fuchsia had never seen before; it was cold and quiet. Arriving at Mr. Neil's ward, they hurried inside. The silence made the noises from the machines reverberate and it seemed as if there were tubes everywhere.

Phantom had received a message from Nurse Nita the previous day. Mr. Neil was one of the old folks from the senior's party the night of the storm. When he took a turn for the worse, his friends somehow got a message out for the group to visit him again. *This must be where life comes to retire*, Fuchsia thought to herself. Fuchsia began to reminisce on the night of the party where she remembered Mr. Neil's dimpled cheeks as he smiled and laughed along with the festivities. It was a stark difference from the man they saw lying eerily still on the hospital bed attached to tubes and machines.

They slowly approached his bed with the same worried expressions spread across their faces.

Shouldn't we just go? Fuchsia thought. But before she could verbalize it, Phantom stepped forward and held Mr. Neil's hand.

"Hello Mr. Neil," she said softly and gently. "It is me, Phantom."

With a couple of moans and groans, Mr. Neil slowly opened his eyes. It seemed to take a moment for him to remember where he was and who they were. He began signalling for the water on the bedside table next to Fuchsia. The wide-eyed stares from the rest of the group prompted her to quickly grab the water and offer him a drink from the straw. He was just another human being lying there, so why did Fuchsia feel so scared? Maybe it was the almost reverent silence. Maybe it was the depressed look on everyone's face. Maybe, it was the realization that Mr. Neil was close to death and it brought back to this usually happy bunch why they were in the hospital in the first place, and how close to death they all were.

It began to dawn on the entire crew that even though they spent lots of time learning about their disease or illness to better understand what was happening to their bodies, no one really spoke of death. Fuchsia remembered the Bible story of Lazarus and how his death was described as "only sleeping". *So why do we fear it so much?* She thought to herself.

The smile on Mr. Neil's face brought Double O 54 back to their purpose. He was so happy he started touching their hands and faces.

The smile on Mr Neil's face suddenly dimmed. "I need your help," he whispered to the group, retrieving a hand-written list that was tucked away under his pillow.

Their eagerness to read the list was curtailed by the voices coming from outside the door. It was time to go. They hugged Mr. Neil and followed Phantom back through pathways only she knew, dodging hospital personnel all the way.

They arrived back at their ward eager to read the list; huddled together, Phantom unfolded the paper.

1. *Go on a rollercoaster*
2. *Have a sleepover with grandchildren*
3. *Sail across the ocean*
4. *Go fishing*
5. *Write a book*

"It's a bucket list!" shouted Sarge.

"A bucket list? What's that?" asked Mac with a puzzled look on his face.

"It's a list of things to do before you die…you know, kick the bucket," Phantom explained.

Mac's eyes widened.

"Poor Mr. Neil. We have to figure out how to help him with this list," Fuchsia pleaded to the group with the image of a sick Mr. Neil lying nearly lifeless on the hospital bed etched in their minds.

There was no way we could get Mr. Neil out of the hospital, Fuchsia thought. *Even if we pretended to be gardeners and pushed him in a wheelbarrow,* as Phantom suggested. She began to wonder why Mr. Neil never did these things with his family. Phantom shared with them that he told her that he was always working and never had time for fun things and that his children and grandchildren seldom visited anymore. *That is very sad. I could not imagine being away from my family. We have to help him, but how?* Fuchsia's mind kept wandering.

Double O 54 was about to give up when Mac had an idea. He told them about something he saw on TikTok, where a dad created a roller coaster for his sick daughter who could not go on a school trip. They decided to give it a try once they had some time alone. They were having so much fun, that Nurse Anita had to come in the room to shush them several times.

So, they had the roller coaster. Next on the list was the sleepover with his grandchildren. They did not know how to contact his real ones, so they decided they could all camp out on his floor for a few hours with a lookout.

"How are we to sail across the ocean and go fishing in a hospital?" said Fuchsia, while going over the list again.

Mac had an idea for that too, so the plan was set.

They timed it perfectly. There was always a lull after visiting hours. When they were sure no one would be looking for them, Phantom led the way to Mr. Neil's room a second time. This time he was up and a smile immediately flashed across his tired but handsome-looking face. While Sarge and Mac set up the activities, Phantom asked him some questions. The answers would not be enough to write a book, but it would document the essence of his life.

Pic set up his easel and started to paint. "They say a picture is worth a thousand words so this will be a wonderful addition," he said proudly as he made the first stroke across the canvas.

They took turns watching the door as they got ready for the roller coaster ride of a lifetime. Fuchsia sat on the bed with Phantom facing the TV screen while Mac and Sarge plugged in a projector and stood behind the bed. As the ride on the screen ascended, they lowered the bed. As the ride began to descend, they raised the bed and as the ride turned corners, they moved the bed to mimic the many turns. They held hands with Mr. Neil as they tried their best to keep in their screams as the euphoria rose. Fuchsia sneaked a look at Phantom who was looking at Mr. Neil. His dimpled-cheeks smile overtook his facial features. He was elated.

Next was the ocean trip. They pretended to be officers on a ship. Mac was the captain. With the bed as their ship, they hoisted the sail–the bedsheet. They dropped anchor–the bedpan. Mac gave Mr. Neil some virtual reality goggles to put on. In virtual reality he was able to cast his net and catch fish, apparently tuna and marlin, which he instructed them to prepare for dinner. They all laughed and shouted, "Aye Aye Captain!"

Soon they could hear the nurses on duty. With swift goodbyes, they gathered their things. They intended on a hasty retreat, but Mr. Neil held their hands as if it was for the last time and said in the most satisfied voice, "Thank you."

The news came the next couple of days that Mr. Neil had passed.

I always thought that was a weird thing to say… someone passed or passed away. Fuchsia thought. *Passed where? Did they not ace the exam of life but only did well enough to move on? Where did they go? I guess it is too hard to say the words 'dead' or 'death'.*

Fuchsia recalled hearing a pastor once say, "Into eternal sleep". She preferred that way of describing it. It made her think of times her dad would go on trips and her mom would say "One more sleep before Dad comes home." That sleep was filled with excitement, not fear.

The funeral was held at the hospital chapel. Some of the nursing staff as well as other older folks came to pay their respects. Fuchsia and the gang watched from the shadows as family members Mr. Neil seldom saw placed beautiful flowers on the coffin. There was a huge picture of him as a young man. Fuchsia thought he was very handsome but serious-looking.

That night Double O 54 held their own little memorial for Mr. Neil. Fuchsia read his story that she had compiled to the others. It spoke about growing up on a farm with stern parents and being laughed at because he always smelled of the farm. It also spoke of him being studious, getting a job in the city, working hard to buy a house and sending his children to the best schools. The main theme was him missing his wife when she died as well as the opportunity to see his grandchildren, and how proud he was of all of them.

They put the painting Pic did on the wall along with the story; he had titled the painting "In Remembrance". It was of a boat in the middle of an ocean just as the sun was setting. They smiled remembering their pretend nautical adventure. As they said a prayer for Mr. Neil's family then opened their eyes, the reality of their existence dawned heavily on them. Could one of them be next?

Fuchsia pictured herself in Pic's painting in the middle of the ocean being lulled to sleep by the gentle waves.

The visual was interrupted by a sudden idea from Phantom. "We should all create a bucket list and keep in touch with a promise to meet if any of us should call."

As they went off to their separate beds with pens and paper to create their bucket lists, Fuchsia began to think about what she would want on her bucket list. Trips to Disney World, skydiving and being an actor in a movie did not seem so important to her now. She looked around, everyone was still up.

"I have another idea!" Fuchsia said out loud, breaking the deafening silence. "Instead of a bucket list, we should promise that when we grew up, we would have careers helping sick children so that they could feel the same sense of family that we have felt here."

Everyone agreed.

Fuchsia quietly said a prayer before bed. "I ask God to be with my family at home and my new hospital family."

As she began to drift off, a sense of calm came over her as a clear direction came to mind of what she wanted to be when she grew up…

If you grow up, the voice in her head countered.

CHAPTER 5

The Phantom Finale: In Remembrance

Fuchsia was not in a hurry; she was tired. She had already attended to several emergencies that day that had left her drained. All she could think of was getting her things together and heading home. She said a quiet prayer as she walked by the wards, reminding God that she was indeed grateful to be alive, for her job as a paediatric therapist and for being able to help enhance the lives of so many critically ill children.

She didn't know why she took the left corridor that day. She seldom held meetings at the hospital but as the last child she saw was in critical care, she made the trip in. A sense of nostalgia flooded her whole being when she walked by Ward 54.

It looked very different with additions such as family suites so families could stay with their little ones, playrooms and even classrooms with computers so that patients could still attend virtual classes if they were up to it.

She found herself strangely drawn to the door. She pushed it half open expecting to see Double O 54 huddled together, planning for their next case. The smile turned into a chuckle that came out before she could stop it. Her mind raced back to them sneaking down corridors and hiding in the closets … the old gang.

After Kevin left, it was not long before Sarge, Mac and Pic got better and went home. Fuchsia and Phantom were the last of the gang. After recovering from her kidney transplant, Fuchsia too went home. That was the last time she saw Phantom.

It was surreal being there. Instead of seeing sickness, the reception area was now lined with beautiful pictures. One in particular was especially eye-catching. It was a boat in the middle of an ocean at sunset. Fuchsia didn't need to read the write-up to know that this was Pic's "In Remembrance". She was so enthralled by this she didn't see the nurse approach her.

"Can I help you, dear? It is beautiful, isn't it? It was donated by one of our patient alumni; they all were. In fact, this wing was refurbished by one too. They had to cancel the opening for the second one because Ms. Atom was not well."

"Did you just say Atom?" Fuchsia looked around so quickly she could have given herself whiplash.

"Well yes. Do you know her? Nice lady, but she's not well. I think she has a suite upstairs."

This must be a sign. Fuchsia's head was suddenly spinning with thoughts of what to do with this information.

"Do you know how I could contact the artist? I would love some pieces for my office?" Fuchsia asked the nurse.

"Well yes. He comes in to do art therapy every week." The nurse went to the computer and after some quick keystrokes, wrote something down on a pink sticky note then gave it to Fuchsia.

"Thank you!" Fuchsia responded, and with that, she headed for the door but instead of the exit, she headed upstairs. She felt positively giddy with excitement at the thought of seeing Phantom again. She found the nurses' station and after much convincing and showing of credentials, one of the nurses pointed down the hallway.

Fuchsia approached cautiously. She opened the door to see a thin but beautiful woman lying on the bed with her eyes closed. Reason then slapped her across the head; how did she not think that she would find Phantom ill? She was so excited that she forgot why people came to the hospital. Before she could take another step, the voice from the bed threatened, "You have five seconds to leave this room, or I will call security." Fuchsia's initial fear was replaced with a smile at the memory of when they first met.

"Five, four, three …" The patient started her countdown and grabbed the phone to show she meant business.

"Oh, stop your bellyaching," Fuchsia said. "Consider me your welcome committee."

"Welcome committee to what, a hospital? Please, there is no such thing. You have two seconds. I am dialling… two, one..."

"Really Phantom, what's the number?"

Phantom smiled as if caught in the lie and Fuchsia rushed to hug her friend.

"It has been a minute since I last heard that name. How is it that you look exactly the same, just grown up?" Phantom asked, taking a look at her friend. She still had short hair, but it was styled in a glamorous pixie cut. "How have you been?"

The two spent the next hour chatting away. They reminisced about the Double O 54 days and the shenanigans their 'gang' got up to. They laughed until they cried when remembering the night Phantom tried to run away and how being in their gang helped them tremendously with their hospital experience. When Fuchsia said that she always thought Nurse Nita had an idea of what was going on, Phantom countered that she was sure that she knew, as her father hired Nurse Nita to be Phantom's private nurse when she left the hospital and they often joked about it.

Phantom sobered a bit as she spoke with joy about her charity work with the hospital. She wanted to make sure that sickness didn't keep children away from families. Soon after, the nurse arrived to take Phantom for some tests. Fuchsia reluctantly said her goodbyes and made her way home thinking about the other gang members and what they were up to.

She didn't have to wait very long. Fuchsia was clad in her flannel PJs and finally heading to bed when the doorbell rang. Who could that be? She knew it wasn't her family because they had done their family check-in via Zoom already for the night. She thought of ignoring it (after all she lived alone), but something about the persistence as the ringing escalated to knocking made Fuchsia throw on her robe and attend to the door.

A peek through the window showed two figures, a man and a child. Instantly alert, she asked suspiciously, "May I help you?"

There was a familiarity to the man as he turned to face the door. "Hi, it's Deacon," he half whispered.

"Deacon who? I don't know anyone by that name." Fuchsia retorted with phone in hand ready to dial 911. This neighbourhood was safe, but she wasn't taking any chances.

The voice outside the door sounded instantly frustrated. "Okay, you must be new. Check your messages from Fantasia," the voice instructed.

Fantasia? Phantom? Fuchsia looked at her phone. It was still on silent from earlier that day and there were loads of messages from an unknown number; it was Phantom. The messages explained that she needed help urgently, that Deacon would come by with the package and that she was to help.

Fuchsia was still apprehensive, but she opened the door. Checking over his shoulder, the man and child entered and closed the door behind them.

It was only in the light of her living room that she realized whom she was talking to. "Sarge?"

At the sound of the name, the man looked at Fuchsia trying to recollect.

"No way! Is this Fuchsia?" He hugged her so hard he lifted her off the ground. "How did Phantom find you?"

"Actually, I found her. I had a client at the hospital and ended up meeting her." Fuchsia responded excitedly.

"Oh, no wonder she wasn't available," Sarge said. "Is she going to be alright?"

"I don't know, to be honest, she looked weak. But I don't understand, what's all this and who is that?" Fuchsia asked, pointing at the little girl who could have been about twelve.

Cecilia

Fuchsia could not believe the story that unfolded. She made up the pull-out couch for the little girl who was obviously fatigued and made some coffee as Sarge explained that in addition to her charity work, Phantom ran a rescue group home for children in need. Children who needed help would call the hotline and she would pick them up; no judgment, no questions asked, but this last case was different.

"The child was basically being held hostage by her family," Sarge explained. "Her younger sister was ill, and her family would use her for parts,'"

Fuchsia shook her head. "Did you say parts?"

"Yes," Sarge confirmed. "The last thing they did was to take her kidney and she almost died."

Sarge was now a private investigator who specialized in finding abducted or run-away children, so Phantom asked him to rescue the little girl whose name was Cecilia.

This was almost too much. Why me? Fuchsia asked herself. As if in answer to her question, her phone rang; it was a private number. *I mean the night couldn't get any stranger, right?* It was a video call from Phantom. She could make out the tubes and machines in the background.

I am so sorry to spring this on you, Fuchsia. I could imagine what you may be thinking." She said. "I am so sorry I couldn't deal with it myself, but this case is different, and after meeting you today, I could think of no one better to help. But how cool it is that the 'Phantom Gang' is together again, right?"

"Double O 54!" Sarge and Fuchsia corrected in unison.

"I don't know what I am supposed to do here, Phantom. Is this even legal?" Fuchsia was genuinely worried and concerned.

Then there was a knock on the door. Sarge jumped up and in one swift movement turned off the light and signalled Fuchsia to be quiet.

Seeing the trepidation on Fuchsia's face, Phantom assured them that they could safely open the door. Sarge took a peek and then smiled.

"No way!" He exclaimed. He opened the door and Kevin stepped inside.

Boys to Men

There were hugs all around. Fuchsia felt unreal seeing these guys after such a long time. Kevin was a lawyer who dealt specifically with minors. Often, he would help Phantom with children in her group home so Phantom could get temporary custody and work with Social Services to help the minor in question.

Phantom left Kevin to fill the group in. Sarge, in true Sarge style, was cooking up something wonderful in the kitchen. If the walls could talk, they would probably say that this was a first.

The group sat at the counter and talked. It was awful what this family was doing to this child. Kevin explained how tricky the law was especially for minors. Usually with Phantom's other clients, if a crime was committed, the court would award Phantom custody. If no crime was committed, the parents would consent, but because Cecilia's parents were not willing to consent, and her records showed that they had a bone marrow surgery planned, Kevin intended to file a petition to emancipate the obviously traumatized child from her parents. It was a long shot, so they decided to hide her until then.

Either the loud chatter or the smell of food

woke Cecilia. Sarge gave her some food. While she wolfed it down, Kevin asked questions to help the case.

Cecilia was scared. Oftentimes therapist Fuchsia had to step in and reassure her and rephrase questions to get her to open up. Kevin had finally gotten an emergency court date and had less than thirty-six hours to find evidence of the trauma she experienced. When Cecilia mentioned that she was usually alone at the hospital, Fuchsia's heart sank. When she mentioned her love for the staff at the hospital and that she gifted her paintings to her art teacher because her family refused to let her keep them, Fuchsia had an idea. She called the number on the pink sticky note.

It was three A.M. when Pic rang her doorbell. He looked like a large version of the little boy with the sketch pad. On seeing him, Cecilia ran to give the familiar face a hug. In his hands were works of art Cecilia had done and after greeting the rest of the group, he showed them the evidence. Fuchsia thought the drawings emitted images of loneliness, hurt and pain in each of them. *How could a parent do this to a child?* Hearing that she seldom went to school and didn't have any friends was even more heart-wrenching. Her biological father died when she was young, and her mother had a hard time conceiving when she remarried. When she finally did conceive, the baby was ill and all the attention, money and resources went to her upkeep. Her new husband no longer wanted Cecilia around and kept her in a room in the basement until they needed something. As a therapist, Fuchsia knew bad things happened, but this was unbelievable.

They worked until the sun came up. The boys made breakfast while Fuchsia helped Cecilia into the bath and some clean clothes. It was amazing that Fuchsia had not seen these guys in ten years and now her house had become ground zero overnight. They must have fallen asleep at some point because they were jolted awake by the sound of the doorbell and Sarge scarily cautioning them to be quiet.

It was the police. The group, hiding behind chairs and counters, deliberated in whispers and hand gestures whether they should open the door. The consensus was no. Fuchsia crouched behind the chair, squeezed her eyes and wished for the police to disappear. She eventually got her wish and Sarge informed them that there was a 'Be On The LookOut' (BOLO) order out for Cecilia.

Apparently, one of Fuchsia's neighbours reported seeing someone matching her description. This prompted them to turn on the news. There was no volume for fear of drawing attention to themselves, but they could see Cecilia's face was all over the headlines. This case was apparently high priority as her stepfather was an influential politician. Fuchsia hated to admit it, but she was getting scared. They still needed concrete evidence of wrongful intent, but first, they needed to get out of there.

They waited until dark and snuck out the back door. If this situation wasn't so scary, Fuchsia would smile at the memory of sneaking around the hospital led by the inevitable Phantom. Her practice seldom involved the authorities and this action of them dressed in dark clothing and under cover of darkness felt criminal.

As they quietly slipped past their neighbours' fences, being careful to stay in the shadows, Fuchsia thought of Phantom. Oh, how she would love this. Fuchsia was so proud of her and the work she was doing, and remembering the pact they made to help children made it even more profound. The trauma of childhood illness was very real. As they waited in the darkness for Sarge to retrieve the car he had cleverly parked blocks away, a small voice told Fuchsia to pray for Phantom, and she did.

Vicks VapoRub

The six of them crowded into the car. Sarge was given clear directions to their next stop. It had to be somewhere that could blend into everyday activity, yet private enough for them to strategize for the next day. The destination did not disappoint. Sarge parked a couple of blocks out and they began to walk in the direction given. This clearly was not the "best" part of town in the traditional sense of the term, but the people on the street seemed pleasant as they greeted them. The group ended up at what looked like a grocery.

They cautiously walked into the store and selected the items specified.

"A can of soup, a package of noodles and, did that read Vicks VapoRub?" The cashier took one look at their haul and asked the camera, apparently, for a price check on the Vicks VapoRub.

As the puzzled group exchanged looks, the phone rang and the cashier instructed them to look at the selection of cough remedies in aisle four. As odd as this seemed, they did that and walked into a doorway that suddenly opened up in front of them. Someone had been watching too much TV again because it seemed as if they had stepped into a time machine. On the other side of the doorway was an office with a wall full of computers and a large desk, behind which sat Mac.

Trepidation turned into joy as the group erupted into smiles at seeing their friend. There were hugs and handshakes all around. Mac looked so different from the little boy in the hospital; Fuchsia was sure they would have passed by him on the street and not even recognized him.

They all took turns telling Mac about the case. His face went from excited, to scared and then mad. Mac then took them to another room that looked like a dorm. He explained that he ran a community center for inner city kids offering camps, free after-school care and homework help in STEM subjects. As most of the kids he helped were from troubled families, there were times when they would need a place to hide until their caretaker got "sober". This allowed them to continue their studies and avoid Child Services unless absolutely necessary. Many of them had gone on to do well and now support the charity.

Fuchsia put Cecilia to bed and as they settled in to focus on the case, had to ask Mac, Why Vicks VapoRub? It turns out that in his culture, people used Vicks as a 'heal-all' rub. You would rub with this super ointment to get rid of any ailment under the sun, perhaps with the exception of a heart attack, and maybe even then. So, one of his first clients would call to say they needed some Vicks VapoRub as a code for help, and it stuck. Fuchsia would never think of Vicks VapoRub the same way again she thought smiling as her mind conjured up an image of the TV ad... "*helps colds, flu, stuffy nose and espionage!*"

The group redirected their focus to the case. Kevin outlined the order. He called them to the 'stand' and briefed them on some of the questions they might be asked, when suddenly there was a scream coming from the dorm room. Thinking the worst, they all rushed in ready to rescue Cecilia. The poor child sat up in fright with sweat drenching her face; she was having a nightmare.

After assuring her that she would be okay and giving her a sip of water, Fuchsia probed her to talk about it. Cecelia described seeing hospital lights and Dr. Shuby with a knife and she got scared. The poor child was traumatized by these surgeries. Fuchsia documented this as evidence of Post-Traumatic Stress Disorder and generalized anxiety and shared this with the rest of the 'legal' team.

"Did you say Dr. Shuby?" Kevin asked suspiciously. "Are you sure Cecelia said Shuby?"

Fuchsia confirmed this. "I have been reviewing the list of paediatric doctors at the hospital and I am pretty sure there is no Shuby," Kevin said, searching through a mountain of paperwork.

"I am there often," Pic agreed, "and I don't know any Shuby either".

"Maybe it is close to another name," Sarge suggested. Kevin pulled the file and split the list so they could all check. There were no names even remotely close.

"Maybe, that's because he does not work at the hospital," Mac said from his computer screen.

"Do you mean like a visiting surgeon?" Fuchsia asked.

"No, like maybe someone who is unlicensed and should not be there." Mac countered looking intently at his screen. Like in the CSI shows, a face appears on a large screen. If he was not licensed how would Cecilia know him as a doctor? The next picture on the screen was a mugshot of Dr. Shuby. Kevin started to get a weird look on his face. This was it, this was what they needed to save Cecilia.

Mac then informed them of Shuby's involvement in paediatric surgery and experimental cell regeneration. It turned out Shuby's medical licence was revoked after a ten-year-old patient died on the operating table but the parents had never given permission for any tests. Shuby theorized that not all bad organs were dead organs and living tissue could be used to regenerate old tissue, therefore alleviating the need for many transplants and resulting in more help for those on a transplant list. However, his "test subjects", all children, had died. It seemed that the test subject he took the organ tissue from had to be young for his theory of tissue regeneration to work. He was even accused of kidnapping homeless children or runaways to be forced as test subjects, and guess which lawyer now turned politician was instrumental in his release? Cecilia's father.

The group took a deep breath. This was almost unbelievable. The next question was how? They figured that Dr. Shuby was taking tissue from Cecilia's organs, but was the hospital involved? A quick search of the records showed that a Dr. Francis was Cecilia's surgeon and thanks to Mac and his 'hackery', they realized that although Cecilia had the scars to prove she had multiple procedures done, there was no hospital record of any surgery. In fact, every time one was scheduled, the records showed that it was cancelled at the last minute, but Cecilia was taken to the operating room anyway. The best they could figure was that the O.R. team would take her to the operating theatre, Dr. Francis would cancel and then Dr. Shuby would do his own surgery while she was there and return her to the wards for post-op care with no one being the wiser but how was that even possible? It was almost morning when they decided to call Phantom.

As early as it was, Phantom answered on the first ring. Mac explained the Shuby theory to her and was shocked to hear what could happen if one had enough money. She told them that Dr. Francis was one of her doctors as a child, a family friend and a huge supporter of her charities, so she could not see him in that role. She put the group on hold and made a call.

Phantom: Dr. Francis, this is Fantasia Atom. I am sorry to call at this time, but this is a matter of life and death.

They all looked at each other in disbelief. Phantom wasted no time.

Dr. Francis: Fantasia? Are you okay?

Phantom: Are you familiar with the Cecilia Townsend case? You are listed as her doctor.

Dr. Francis: You know I can't disclose a patient's care with you Fantasia.
Phantom: You can discuss it with me, or with the police as you will be implicated in the case.
Dr. Francis: What case? Do you think I kidnapped her?

Phantom then explained their theory; if the Doctor was asleep before, he was definitely alert now.

Dr. Francis: No! You have it all wrong. Several times her parents would complain of some ailment. With the supporting documents from the family doctor, I would run some tests then schedule an exploratory surgery at their request and then, at the last minute, they would cancel. This happened three or four times. Are you saying that someone else did those surgeries?
Phantom: Not just someone else, a Dr. Shuby.
Dr. Francis: You mean their family doctor? That Dr. Shulby?

This explained a lot.

Phantom: I am going to need you to testify to this.

Dr. Francis agreed, eager to set the record straight.

Cecilia Too

With morning light sneaking through the blinds, the exhausted team got ready and headed to court where they nervously sat behind Kevin and Cecilia.

Within an hour, the courtroom was full. Although there were no photos to be taken due to the fact that Cecilia was a minor, it was full of reporters. When Cecilia's parents arrived, they sat glaring at Kevin from the opposite side of the room. As if on cue, Mrs. Townsend started to cry and accused him of stealing her baby and tried calling Cecilia to her. This publicity stunt got the room chattering until the judge arrived and pounded the gravel for order.

It was a long and arduous case with the judge trying to make sense of the situation. Fuchsia felt impatient and had visions of herself shaking him like a rag doll, but she knew this was not how justice was served.

It was almost lunch when Cecilia asked where her sister was. It then dawned on Fuchsia that they didn't know much about her sister. If Cecilia was having surgeries to harvest her organs for her sister, then her sister would need to have surgeries too. Yet, Pic confirmed that he never saw the sister at the hospital. Fuchsia tried to comfort Cecelia and asked for her sister's name.

She said her sister's name was Alia. "Well it is really Cecilia too, but we call her Alia for short." Cecilia clarified. Her answer sent a shiver up Fuchsia's spine.

In none of the testimony did the parents reveal they had another daughter. In fact, several times their lawyer alluded to mental health issues and that Cecilia needed special care. Yet, none of the news reports ever mentioned the Townsends having another daughter. The only person who ever mentioned another daughter was Cecilia. Was she making this up? Fuchsia put Mac and his hackery on the case; he pulled them aside during recess.

There was no record of a second Cecilia, Mac revealed to the utter confusion of the others. There were doctor notes on several pregnancies, miscarriages and deaths, but there was no record of Mrs. Townsend ever conceiving a second child. They were floored. Fuchsia spoke with Cecilia again. She was certain the child wasn't faking, after all, the pictures she had drawn had two children in them. Why would their parents name both of them Cecilia?

The answer came from Cecilia herself, "So that when I go to heaven, mummy would have another better Cecilia". This case was getting weirder by the minute. Every time they started to figure things out, there was another knot to unravel.

It was time for them to head back into the courtroom. During Kevin's address to the bench, they could see the disbelief on the judge's face as they mentioned Cecilia being "used for parts". Dr. Francis was then called to the stand. As he walked in from the waiting room, he looked at the group in disbelief. *What is going on here? Did he change his mind about testifying?* Fuchsia thought, He motioned for Kevin who immediately asked for another recess. The judge wasn't happy but because it was a minor, it was granted.

"That's not Cecilia." Dr. Francis exclaimed when they were together in private. "That's not the child I examined, that's not her!"

What? The group was floored once again. The more they tried to finish the puzzle the more elusive the end was. Dr. Francis then described a child that looked like Cecilia but was younger.

"That's Alia," Cecilia clarified, causing more confusion among the group.

It was time to return to court. They knew they had something, but what? It all became clear when Sarge and Pic returned in the nick of time with

Phantom. Behind them was a tiny version of Cecilia.

It turned out that Cecilia number two called the hotline because she couldn't find her sister. Phantom discharged herself from the hospital to rescue her and was able to put the pieces together. When Cecilia's mother couldn't bring the children to term, their doctor, Dr. Shulby told them about a way to save their babies. The next pregnancy was a secret. Dr. Shulby delivered the baby and began the plot to keep it alive at all costs; this involved taking small portions of Cecilia's number one's organs. As the Cecilias started to grow up, it was more and more difficult to keep a healthy child, hide scars, and to get medication, so they started to home-school her.

They would take Cecilia number two in for check-ups to see what was wrong, using Cecilia number one's documents to book appointments and to get medication. Once a problem was identified, they would book Cecilia number one for surgery, cancel with the real doctor after she was taken to the O.R. and have Dr. Shulby and Cecilia number two come in through the back for the surgeries, probably dressed as a guard or orderly. Cecilia number one would be returned to the ward and discharged quickly because of who her father was. None of the nurses asked any questions and no one knew there were two Cecilias.

The look on their parent's faces, when the group returned to the courtroom with the 'Cecilias' in tow, told them that their story was on point. The Townsends tried to drop the case, saying it was a misunderstanding and that Cecilia could have her emancipation. This took even their lawyer by surprise. The confused judge had no choice but to call all parties into his chambers.

You could hear a pin drop when they returned. He cleared the courtroom of everyone except the lawyers, the plaintiff and the defendant. All the news agencies were buzzing around outside, updating the news feed and trying to figure out what was going on. After about thirty minutes, the Townsends emerged in handcuffs and were hurried away by the police. The news agencies were so confused they crowded them, each reporter clamouring and fighting to get a comment.

After the crowd dissipated, Phantom emerged with the Cecilias in hand. The judge ruled that Cecilia number one was too young for emancipation but that both Cecilias will remain wards of the state with Phantom as their legal guardian. In Addition, the Townsend estate would be sold, and the proceeds put in a trust fund for the girls. This was excellent news. To avoid the paparazzi, the guards allowed Fuschia and the gang to exit through another door.

They recuperated at Phantom's that night. They still could not believe what had happened in the last few days. Every news agency was running the story of the politician and his wife who were arrested on several counts of child endangerment and fraud, and of the pending arrest of Dr. Shulby who apparently was on the run and headed to Mexico.

It occurred to Fuchsia that if these children were to have a normal life that they had a lot of work to do, and first on that list was getting their identities on track. Kevin filed the paperwork right away and Fuchsia had the pleasure of putting Cece and Alia Atomborough to bed. They both loved the story Fuchsia told them of Double O 54 sneaking out of the hospital that fateful day, and the fact that they were now part of their special family.

Fuchsia stood in the doorway and watched as Sarge, Mac, Pic, Kevin and Phantom chatted and joked with each other. Just for a minute, they were all back in the hospital room in their hospital gowns attached to tubes and walkers, worrying about what the future would hold.

How many times over the years had they thought of how close to death they were and how this friendship shaped who they have become? What they did today was nothing short of amazing. Fuchsia loved her job but never had this feeling of doing real good before.

"How about if this were permanent?" Fuchsia hadn't even realized she had said it out loud until everyone stopped and looked in her direction.

"Are you being nostalgic, Fuchsia?" Phantom asked. "Maybe you are right. Maybe we should make the Phantom Gang permanent."

"Double 0 54!" They all corrected in unison.

Meet the Author

"Learning is best done when children are curious, engaged, active, confident, and successful." Author, playwright and educator Fern Best has been creating the ideal environment for this by using stories as a medium to bring concepts to life, particularly within the primary education setting. Primary is where Fern spent most of her teaching career in her home country of Barbados, encouraging a love for writing, theatre arts and culture, and fostering their integration into the learning.

Meet the Author

"Learning is best done when children are curious, engaged, active, confident, and successful." Author, playwright, and educator Fern Best has been creating the ideal environment for this by using stories as a medium to bring concepts to life, particularly within the primary education setting. Primary is where Fern spent most of her teaching career in her home country of Barbados, encouraging a love for writing, theatre arts and culture, and fostering their integration into the learning experience. Today, Fern lives with her family in Canada and works in higher education. She recently scripted Annalisa, this play was produced by the John McCrae Primary School in Markham Ontario and was well received by the school community. Annalisa has since been converted into an audiobook. This has reignited Fern's love of writing and she is now in the process of publishing several pieces of work.

Meet the Artist

Nishani Dahoma is an 18-year-old painter, illustrator and digital artist from the island of Barbados. She aspires to create art that showcases the beauty of Caribbean culture while expressing the ideas she loves. She has received two gold awards and one silver for her NIFCA visual arts submissions in 2023.

Contact: ndahoma.art@gmail.com